A Zat?
What's That?

To: Scarlett
Merry Christmas
♡ Rozzie
December
2020

Jonell Hart

Jonell Hart
Illustrated by Terry Castellani

www.fiandbooks.com

First published in UK in 2020 by Fiona Woodhead from FiandBooks.com
67 The Hollins, Triangle, Halifax, West Yorkshire. HX6 3LU. UK.
www.fiandbooks.com

Paperback ISBN ISBN 978-1-7358219-0-0

Hardback ISBN 978-1-7358219-1-7

This book is dedicated to:
Sara Beth, Charlie, John David and Annie.

My grandchildren and four
big pieces of my heart.

A Zat came into the house today.

It got on my shoe when I went out to play.

When I came inside, it came in, too.
I didn't know it was on my shoe!

I didn't even know
we had a Zat.

We have a dog.
We have a cat...

My brother's gerbil,

And my little sister's turtle.

Pets with two legs, pets with four,
But Zats, I guess, have a whole lot more.

It crawled across the kitchen rug:
Kind of a mouse, but kind of a bug.

It has some fur, and tiny eyes.
And pretty big ears
for a thing
that size.

My mom was
screaming,
"Catch that thing!
Be careful!
I hope it doesn't sting!"

I chased it, but it ran away.
Those Zats are FAST! I have to say!

I chased it through the living room.
My mom came running
in with a broom.

I picked him up from behind the chair,
And lifted him up into the air.

I touched his tiny legs and eyes
While Mom just stood there in surprise!

"You'll have to take him out now, dear. I hope there are no others near."

We opened the door to go outside.
My mother's eyes opened really wide!

Another Zat was by the door,
And in the yard, a whole lot more!

I walked out slowly, Zat in hand.
And put my Zat on a pile of sand.

All the others gathered round.
Lots of Zats were on the ground!

I said to Mom, "What do we do?" She said,
"Don't get them on your shoe!"

Can you guide the Zat to the shoes?